Living with Lucy

Mike Ragland

illustrated by Judith Johnson Frasure

[signature: Mike Ragland]

[signature: Judith Frasure]

Living With Lucy

ISBN: 978-0-9909746-9-7 (print)
978-0-9983261-9-4 (ebook)

Library of Congress Control Number: 2016958018

edited by: Ann Driscol
interior design: Dekie Hicks
cover design and art by: Judith Johnson Frasure

wheredepony

Wheredepony Press
Rome, GA 30165

printed in the United States of America

This book is dedicated with love and affection to all the people who spend their time and money rescuing and finding homes for dogs and cats.

And, of course, to **Dachshund Lovers** everywhere!!

Acknowledgements

There is no way to list everybody who helped me with this book, either by being a reviewer, or providing inspiration. I do feel indebted to each and every one. A few of those are:

My chocolate Dachshund, *LUCY.*

As I began posting my conversations with Lucy on social media, several folks said I needed to put them together in a book and I took it to heart. One of the first was **Ken Dudley**.

My wife, **Martha**, my sounding board, who listens patiently to my ideas and complaints.

I pitched the idea of illustrations and covers to **Judith Johnson Frasure**, one of Rome's foremost artists. She was excited about the project and added way more than just her beautiful creations.

Ann Calloway Driscol, who edited this effort. I depend on her heavily to straighten out all my errors.

Kathy Stephens Jones, who intercepted all the Lucy conversations from social media, emailed them by date so I could keep them in some form of order until it came time to write.

Margaret Hollingsworth, who takes care of my web page and all things computerized.

Dekie Hicks, who published all my books.

Author's Note

The story of Lucy the Chocolate Dachshund began when she came to live with us in Cave Spring. She was a six week old puppy, trying to adjust to a new family.

She enjoys being an ordinary puppy. She has no desire to be famous, or a celebrity of any kind, although she could be the most famous of them all.

Lucy has one unique trait that sets her apart from all other Dachshunds. She can talk. She is fluent in English, German, and French.

She has no idea where she learned those languages. There are certain things she knows, and has no idea where they came from. But Lucy still has to learn the simple things that every puppy has to learn the hard way.

She refuses to talk to anyone other than me. She is afraid she would be exploited and forced to live in a crate, in a government laboratory. She says it's ok for me to tell her story, seeing as how I'm a writer. No one would believe me anyway, and she's right.

Table of Contents

Chapter 1
Living with Lucy

I sat and watched Gertie the Dachshund get off her bed in front of the fireplace and walk to the front door. She crossed the porch and eased down the steps. She spent ten or fifteen minutes in the front yard, then came back up the steps and into the house. Her red color was turning white in places. Her nose, around her eyes, and front feet were almost white from age. I was thinking. How old is she?

The best I could remember she would be around ten years old. She should still have a few good years left, but she sure was showing her age.

My wife Martha loved Gertie as much as any pet we've ever had. Gertie shared our house with three cats and an outside dog named Sophie. But she was a favorite. If something happened to Gertie, I don't know what Martha would do.

I watched Gertie poking around for a few days, then had an idea. I called my daughter Bekki and told her my plan. She is also a Dachshund lover and has two of her own—a Black and Tan named Gretchen and a Chocolate named Memphis.

I told Bekki we needed to be thinking about getting another Dachshund to spend some time with Gertie, and to let Martha fall in love with a new puppy.

I knew it was a mistake the minute I called. Start thinking to her meant right now.

"Daddy, I'll call Kathy and see if she is going to have any puppies anytime soon," she said.

What could I do? I was boxed in. I had painted myself into a corner.

"Well, go ahead," I said. "Tell her to let us know the next time her Mama dog is expecting."

Kathy is my niece. She lives in Ellijay and her beautiful female Dachshund has a litter of puppies every year. One of my daughter's Dachshunds came from Kathy, so I knew when her puppies were available they would be pretty.

Bekki called me the next day.

"Kathy has two puppies right now," she said. "They were born on July 21st and are ready to go. I'm going to meet her in Calhoun and get one of them for Mama's birthday."

Martha's birthday was September the 8th. This was the end of August. Once again I was boxed in. It was kind of like fate had dealt me a losing hand.

The following Sunday, Bekki came to the house with this little wiggling six-week old Chocolate female. We named her Lucy. She became a lap puppy in no time at all.

Dachshunds are still hound dogs. They came from Germany, and were bred as badger hounds. There aren't any badgers in Georgia to chase or dig out of burrows, plus they became too cute and were soon just pets. But they still have a hound dog face, and can look so sad. This little puppy would sit in my lap and just about break my heart looking at me.

I would sit and hold her, wondering what she was thinking. She would move her mouth like she was chewing on something. I'd check and see she didn't have anything in her mouth.

Then I began to hear Martha call my name when she was in a back room. I would walk to the other part of the house and ask what she wanted.

"Nothing," she said. "I didn't call you."

"I heard you," I said, "loud and clear."

"You didn't hear me," she said. "You're losing it, buster. Cause I haven't called you."

I would return to my chair, thinking I may be losing it. I've heard about people hearing voices, and none of it was good. An hour or two later "Hey Mike" would sound out from a back room. Once again I would ask what Martha wanted. And once again I got the same answer.

Several days later it was time to take Lucy to the vet for her first set of puppy shots. I put her in a cat carrier, placing her in the passenger seat where I could see through the mesh screen and make sure she was all right. She didn't like it. She whined and howled. Just like a hound dog puppy.

About half way to the vet I heard a voice.

"Hey, fat boy," the voice said. "Where are we going?"

I tried to ignore it, but couldn't. I broke out in a sweat, began breathing rapidly, and could feel my heart begin to fly.

I'm having an anxiety attack. What to do? Usually, I'd begin to read. Reading anything would change my channel and stop the attack. But I can't read and drive.

"Are you deaf?" the voice asked. "I asked you, where are we going?"

I looked down and Lucy was looking straight at me.

Oh Lord, Oh Lord, the voice is coming from the puppy. I'm hearing voices from a dog. Human voices too. I've been working too hard. I need rest. That's not right. I'm retired and don't work at all. I just write books and stories. Maybe that's work. No, it isn't to me. I enjoy it. I'm just old and going crazy. They'll put me in the "P" wing at the hospital if they find out. I'm rambling, I can't help it.

"Are you going to answer or not?" asked the voice.

"We're going to the vet," I said. "Lord, I'm talking back to a dog. I'm answering a voice from a puppy. Please help me."

"What's a vet?" asked the puppy.

"It's a doctor for animals," I said.

"You got a sick pet there?" she asked.

"No, I'm taking you," I said.

"For what?" she asked. "I'm not sick."

"You have to be checked over, it's a wellness exam," I said as we pulled into Lakeview Animal Clinic, "and get your first set of shots."

They know me at Lakeview. Dr. Johnson has been taking care of my animals for years. But they don't know Lucy. Mary, the receptionist, opened a file on Lucy and we saw the Doc.

Afterwards, I put Lucy back in the cat carrier and we headed home.

"I hope you enjoyed that," she said.

"Enjoyed what?" I asked.

"Taking me to the vet," she said. "I ain't going ever again."

"Yes, you are," I said. "In three weeks we come back."

"Mike," she said. "That is your name, isn't it? Mike."

"Yep, that's me," I said.

"I have a mom, a dad, and a brother," she said. "It's a nice home. Then the lady that lives there gets me, puts me in a car, and drives me to where another lady meets us. They just toss me in another car and bring me to your place. Your house has an old Dachshund that can barely get around and a million cats. It's not too bad, although I'm lonely for my family. Then, after a couple of days you bring me here."

"Just trying to take care of you," I said. "If you don't get your shots, you could get real sick, and maybe die."

"What are you talking about?" Lucy asked. "Stabbing me with a needle is going to keep me from getting sick? And what was that stuff she squirted down my throat?"

"It was worm medicine," I said. "To get rid of worms if you have any."

"Worms!" she yelled pretty loudly for a puppy. "I don't have worms. Why don't they check before putting stuff in your mouth?"

"You wouldn't like the way they check," I told her. "They take a stool sample to see if you have worms."

"What is that?" she asked.

"They run this little rod up your behind until they get a sample," I explained, "then check it under a microscope."

"You better never let them do that to me." she said. "And I didn't need shots."

"Yes, you did," I said. "There are a lot of bad puppy dis-

4

eases. Shots help prevent them."

"What kind of diseases?" she wanted to know.

"There's a lot," I said. "But Parvo and Distemper have killed a lot of puppies. You got the first set of those shots today."

"First set?" she mumbled. "You mean there's more?"

"Yes, there is."

"Well, the worm medicine didn't taste too bad," she said. "What does cutting part of my toes off have to do with preventing disease?"

"I saw you squirming," I said. "That was uncalled for."

"I'll bet if you were having your toes amputated, you'd squirm too."

"Dr. Johnson just clipped your nails," I informed her. "Long nails cause you to walk funny. It also strains the leg muscles and torques the spine. Last thing a Dachshund needs is more back problems. Nails can grow into the bottom of your foot and get infected and be painful."

"Well, I still don't like it," she said. "I ain't going no more."

"Yes, you are," I said. "You're just a little puppy and are going to go."

"I'll bet you didn't go to a doctor when you were little and get shots," she said, looking up at me.

"I'll bet I did," I said. "And when I went overseas, we got a bunch, all at the same time."

"Oooh," she barked her little puppy bark. "Did you go to Germany?"

"Nah," I said. "But I did go to France."

Aww d'etre en France au printemps, she said.

"What was that?" I asked.

"Nothing," she said softly. "I was just thinking."

"Now it's my time," I said. "How are you able to talk?"

"I don't know," she said. "I just can. I realized I could understand you and Grandma."

"Grandma," I said. "You mean Martha?"

"The other guy that lives here calls her Grandma," she said. "It's easy for me to say. I could make voices from my throat. It just took me a while to be able to speak. Then I realized that I could understand other languages, and speak them too."

"Yeah, I heard French a bit ago," I said. "What else?"

"*Ich kann sprechen Deutsche*," she said.

"That's German," I said.

"I'm a German descendent," she said.

"I am too on one line," I said.

"Mike, maybe you had a witch in your lineage," she said.

"I did," I said. "But would that give me a talking dog?"

"Not sure," she said. "What did the witch do?"

"Poisoned some kids," I said, "and put curses on animals. You know cows, sheep, goats, horses and maybe others."

"What happened to her?" she asked.

"They beheaded her with a sword, and burned her at the stake," I said. "She said she didn't do it. But during torture she admitted to being a witch."

"Where was this?" she asked.

"In Alsace," I answered, "back in 1673."

"Alsace," she whispered to herself. Then aloud she said, "It has always been a disputed piece of property between Germany and France. And I can speak both languages. That might be your answer. Then, it might not be."

"No way," I said. "You didn't come to me from a witch. We'll know in due time what your purpose is, but it ain't from no witch."

As we pulled into the driveway she looked at me. "No talking in front of others. Do you understand?"

"Do I have a choice?" I asked.

"None at all," she said. "I'm a happy Dachshund. There's a lot I need to learn, and I want you to teach me."

Chapter 2
Lucy Goes to the Park

We went back to the vet every three weeks for three more trips. During that time, Lucy sat in my lap a lot. She loved for me to read my morning devotional out loud. She became interested in the Bible stories I began to read to her. There were times she came up with her own interpretation, or changed one to fit her way of thinking.

We watched a lot of football. She became a big Alabama fan, and would do a "Roll Tide" when grandma wasn't around. The fast cars of NASCAR just fascinated her. She was a big Danica Patrick fan. She liked the idea of a female competing with all the guys. But after Danica wrecked her car, Lucy would quit watching and find some Dachshund thing to do, or something to tear up.

One afternoon I had Martha put the harness on Lucy. I got the Dachshund's leash and she began running in circles. She knew we were going somewhere. She hated going to the vet, but loved riding in the car.

"Hey Mike," she said as we settled down inside, "I thought we were through with the vet."

"We don't have to for awhile," I said. "You've now had your rabies shot. So we're going to the park for a walk. I think you'll like it."

"What did the rabies shot have to do with it?" she wanted to know.

"Sometimes certain wild animals infected with rabies come around and attack other animals," I said. "Then the animals catch rabies and have to be destroyed. Now you're safe."

"What about you?" she asked. "Have you had your rabies shot?"

"People don't have to have them till something with rabies bites them," I said.

We got out at the park and Lucy went nuts. She began jumping, running behind me, then to the end of the leash in front. Smelling every stick and leaf, she held her head high in the air reading the wind currents. We started around the half mile circle through the park and had almost finished the first lap when we came to the Cave Lake. Standing in front of us were four beautiful Canada geese.

When Lucy saw them I could almost feel the skid marks as she applied the brakes. She stared at them for a few minutes. They didn't move.

"Mike," she said. "What are those things?"

"They're geese," I said.

"What do they do?" she asked.

"They swim in the lake," I said. "They eat a lot of small fish, and fly around visiting other lakes and rivers. They also eat a lot of seed and grain."

"What are they good for?" she asked, keeping her eyes glued to the big gander.

"A lot of folks hunt them in season," I said. "Some people like to eat them."

"Will they bite?" she asked.

"They can," I said, "but I don't think they will."

"Why?" she asked. "They're looking mean at me."

"They don't like dogs," I said.

"I don't like them," she told me. "Make them go away."

"Let's ease up closer and see if they don't just get in the lake and swim away."

"Are you sure?" she asked.

"Of course," I said. "Didn't I tell you the squirrel we saw earlier would run up a tree?"

"You did," she said. "Then you thought for some reason I should sit at the base of the tree and look up at the ugly thing."

"Most Dachshunds do," I said.

"I ain't most Dachshunds," she said. "Haven't you figured that out yet?"

Lucy began to ease toward the four geese blocking the trail. As she got a little closer she turned to me and said,

"Those things are four times bigger than I am. Don't you let them bite me!"

As we walked by, the geese eased into the lake and swam out about ten feet.

"Whew, that was close," she said, moving on down the trail. "What are those people doing up ahead?"

"Getting water from the cave," I said. "It's the best water anywhere around. A lot of folks come to dip a few gallons. It has no chemicals of any kind as it bubbles up from the ground. The water fell as rain a hundred years ago."

"What's in the cave?" she wanted to know.

"The ghost of a wolf. And a few of his friends," I said.

"I'm not going in there," she said.

"Are you chicken?" I asked.

"Look. I'm not even six months old," she declared. "I'm planning on getting a little older. I'm not messing with a wolf. Or ghosts."

As we pulled into the driveway she wanted to know if we could go to the park every day.

"That was fun, Mike," she said.

"Not every day," I said. "We can go a lot, though, if you like."

"I do," she said. "It gets boring being in the house all the time."

Chapter 3
Lucy Tries Vegetables

"Hey Mike," Lucy said, looking up from the floor. "The dry dog food is getting pretty dry. How about a treat? Or some canned stuff?"

"All the folks on Facebook tell me you don't need them," I said. "I've got something else I want you to try."

"What?" she asked. "Am I the experiment Dachshund? Why not give it to Gertie?"

I gave Lucy a baby carrot. She loved it, and wanted another. Then Gertie the Dachshund wanted one. She liked the carrot too. So now I'm learning. Dachshunds like baby carrots.

The next day after I came in from church, I peeled a banana. Another person told me that Dachshunds also liked bananas. I pinched off an inch and put it in Lucy's dish. She looked at it, gave it a lick, then turned to me, asking "What is that?"

"It's a banana," I said.

"It's nasty," she said, running around coughing and acting like she was choking. "Where do they come from?"

"From the jungles," I said. "Monkeys love them."

"Do I look like a monkey?" she asked.

"No," I said. "But you're acting like one."

"Listen Mike." She looked at me. "Give me something good to eat, and you eat the monkey food. It suits you."

An hour later I put the banana in the garbage, and she didn't get a treat after all.

Chapter 4
Lucy Meets Christy and Learns about Ghosts

On a day in late September, Lucy and I were in the park walking. We stopped to let a car pass at the road near the pool. We were on our fourth lap, and I didn't mind the stop a bit.

After we got back home Lucy was perched in my lap when she asked, "Mike, who was the pretty lady in the black car at the park?"

"That was Christy Davis," I said.

"The one that got out of the car and petted me," she confirmed.

"That was Christy," I said. "I noticed you pee'd all over her foot while she was petting you. Why do you do that?"

"I don't mean to," she said. "Just can't help myself. What does she do?"

"She's a teacher," I said. "She's also in charge of all of the city's ghost events. That's what she and Barry were doing in the park. They were getting ready to go ghost hunting."

"Ask her if she'll take me," Lucy said. "I want to see a ghost. Maybe I'd see a ghost Dachshund."

"You'd be scared," I told her. "And you'd run and hide. You'd probably turn half white."

"I still want to go," she said. "Will you ask her?"

"Will you promise not to pee on her?" I asked.

"I promise to try not to," she said.

"OK, I'll ask her that. I'm going to write the story."

"Lots of people and dogs are scared of ghosts," Lucy said. "Don't you remember how scared Scooby was, and he was a big boy dog?"

"Yeah, he was a Great Dane," I said. "I'll ask her. But the other day you wouldn't go in the cave because of the ghost wolf. Have you changed your mind?"

"Nope," she said. "I'm just older now."

Chapter 5
Autumn 2015
Lucy Learns Why Trees Shed Leaves and about Halloween

"Hey Mike," Lucy the Dachshund said, coming over to the chair where I was sitting. "Something is happening to this tree. Some of its leaves are falling off, and the others don't look too healthy."

"We're in the first week of October," I said. "It's autumn now. Most of the trees will shed their leaves after they turn pretty different colors. Just wait a few weeks, and you'll see big changes on the mountainsides and in the park."

"Why do they do that?" she asked. "Shed their leaves and all."

"The green in the leaves is caused by an abundance of chlorophyll," I said. "It takes a lot of sunlight to keep the trees in chlorophyll. As winter approaches, the days are shorter and the sun isn't as bright. It would take a lot of energy for a tree to keep its leaves. It's easier on it to just grow new ones in the spring when the days start getting longer."

"That seems too simple," she said. "There must be more to it than just sunlight."

"Of course there is," I said. "But you just got the little girl answer."

"Then why don't pine trees lose their needles?" she asked.

"I knew that was coming," I said. "They do, just not all at one time. They lose some every month. The new needles push the old ones out of the tree. In the fall they keep about half their needles to capture sunlight (food). They're evergreen trees, not deciduous ones. In other words, they're different kinds of trees."

"Letting the big words fly now, aren't you," she commented. "I know big words too. Like Halloween, watermelon, elephant."

"Do you know what they mean?" I asked.

"I know what a watermelon is," she said. "I like them. And I know what an elephant is too. But what is Halloween?"

"It's a day when witches, ghosts, goblins, and trolls all come out and move around town 'trick or treating' folks," I said.

"What does trick or treating mean?" she asked.

"They ask for treats at every door," I said. "And they have a bag for you to drop them in."

"I don't want them to come to our house," she said. "I don't have enough now. You run them off, Mike."

"What are you going to do when they come by?" I asked.

"I'm going to be sitting in your lap," she said.

Chapter 6
Lucy Meets Abigail and Pookie

Several days before Cave Spring's annual Ghost Walk, I thought I would go to the park and time the walk. Our leader was limiting the story tellers to about ten minutes per stop. I was the fifth stop. I wanted to see how long it would take before the first group got to me. I knew after that it would be non-stop till around 10:30 or 11:00 pm. I had no idea how many groups there would be.

Last year we had a stream of groups in the Ghost Walk. They consisted of around forty per group for almost four hours. I harnessed Lucy the Dachshund up and to the park we went.

"Hey Mike," said Lucy. "I've never been here in the dark before. What are we doing?"

"Just checking out the trail for the Ghost Walk," I said.

"Are you going to have real ghosts on the walk?" she asked. "Or just stories."

"We're going to have real stories," I said. "But a lot of folks have seen strange things on our walks in the past."

"Like what?" she asked.

"Like seeing faces in the windows of Fannin Hall," I said. "And mist in the cave wrapping around folks' legs, and climbing up them till it got to their watch."

"You're scaring me," she declared. "Let's go home."

"Don't you want to go in the cave," I said as we walked by the entrance.

"No, you said there was the ghost of a wolf in there," she said pulling harder on her leash. "I don't want to see a wolf of any kind."

As we neared the playground, Lucy stopped.

"Hey Mike," she said. "What is the little girl doing over in front of that house?"

"What little girl?" I asked. "I don't see a little girl."

"Are you blind?" she asked. "She's looking for something. Can't you see her?"

"No, I can't," I replied.

"It's a cat!" barked Lucy. "She's looking for her cat, and it's hiding from her."

"Do you see the cat?" I asked.

"Yes. It's hiding behind a bush," she said.

We were near the yard of the Hearne Inn when Lucy asked me to turn her loose. "Let me go Mike," she said. "I'll show her where the cat is hiding."

I unsnapped the leash and Lucy took off in a run toward the Inn. She went around the bushes several times and then back to the front of the steps. She was sitting on her back legs like a prairie dog, tail just a-wagging.

She rolled around on the ground for a few minutes then came back to where I was waiting. I snapped on her leash.

"Are you finished?" I asked.

"Yep," she answered. "She got her cat and went back inside."

"Why were you rolling around in the driveway?" I asked. "You looked silly."

"Mike, she was petting me," Lucy said. "Didn't you see her?"

"No, I didn't," I said. "And I didn't see a door open for her to go inside."

"She didn't open a door," Lucy said. "She just walked right through."

"Did she tell you her name?" I asked.

"She said her name was Abigail," Lucy replied. "And she asked me what my name was?"

"And the cat's name?" I asked.

"I heard her call it Pookie as she picked her up to go inside," Lucy said.

"Come on, girl," I said, heading for the car. "Let's go home."

On the way home I was thinking about Abigail and Pookie. I heard a lot about Abigail from the ladies at City Hall. She did live there at one time. I was wondering if she had moved after our renovation of Fannin Hall, where our City offices were, or was she just visiting in the park.

Christy Davis, of Southern Paranormal Investigators, had mentioned Pookie to me recently.

How would Lucy have known those names unless she was petting her, and Lucy could see Abigail? It's something to think about.

Chapter 7

Lucy Likes the Harmonica And Learns Not to Make Fun of Other People

"What were you doing on the porch?" Wife asked. "Lucy was having a fit, thought she'd lost you."

"While I was hunting the car keys I lost the other day," I said, "I found my old blues band harmonica. I've been threatening to dig it out, but didn't know where it was."

"Could you still make it work?" she asked.

"Actually, I remembered more than I thought I would," I said, playing just a little of Amazing Grace, Shenandoah, and then a poor imitation of a train.

Lucy was running around in circles, and Gertie was sitting on her back legs like a prairie dog, bobbing up and down.

"They like it," said Wife. I don't think they want you to stop."

I turned and walked into the office, placing the little harmonica in a dish on my desk. Lucy was right behind me.

"Hey Mike," she said. "Why did you quit? Gertie and I liked that song."

"I thought it was hurting your ears," I said.

"No, it tickles them," she said with a doggie's grin. "Gertie said you used to play the harmonica when she was a puppy."

"I guess it's been that long," I said. "I had a couple more in different keys. I gave them to a homeless man on Broad Street in Rome. He was good, and could play some blues."

"I got an idea, Mike," Lucy said.

"I'm afraid to ask," I said. "But I will. What is it?"

"You know the old black cowboy hat in the back seat of the Cadillac," she said. "Get it and those wrap-around dark sunglasses the eye doctor told you to wear after your eye surgery."

"And," I said.

"We go to the park, you sit on a bench," she said. "Put them on, start playing a little blues."

"That's not funny," I told her. "I can't play the blues, at least not good. But if you danced around like a monkey, folks wouldn't notice me."

"Well, let's go then," she said. "I'll do it."

"You're a bad dog," I said. "You just want to go to the park. When the housekeeper comes tomorrow I'm going to have her get after you with the vacuum cleaner."

"Somebody's going to get bit," she said running toward the bedroom and yelling back at me. "Hey Mike, can you bend a note, hehehe."

"No, I can't!" I yelled after her. "No more treats for you."

Chapter 8
Lucy Gets Her Feelings Hurt

"Hey Mike, I want to ask you something," said Lucy the Dachshund.

"What is it?" I asked.

"On the way home from Rome yesterday you had the radio on," she said.

"Yes, I did," I said. "Thought you liked the radio."

"It's OK," she said. "I don't understand why that man was yelling at his dog and calling it names."

"What man?" I asked. "It was a classic Rock 'n Roll station."

"He kept saying his dog wasn't nothing but a Hound Dog," she said. "And cries all the time."

"It's just a song, Lucy," I said.

"Well, I don't like it," she replied. "Mike, have you ever caught a rabbit? It's hard to do. And for him to say his dog wasn't a friend because he couldn't catch a rabbit is mean."

"I told you it was just a song," I said. "And it's an old one at that. Forget about it."

"Do you think I'm high class, Mike?" she asked.

"Sure I do," I answered. "Why?"

"That man said folks thought his dog was high class, but it was a lie," she said. "I feel sorry for his dog."

"Well, you're high class," I said.

"Dang right," she replied. "How many folks have a talking Dachshund?"

"I don't know of any," I said. "What brought all of this on?"

"You call me a hound dog," she said. "Just like the man on the radio."

"You're a good little hound dog," I said.

"And I don't have to catch rabbits for us to be friends?" she asked.

"Not a one," I said.

"That's good," she said. "I don't like the song. It's depressing."

"Lucy," I said. "I never thought about it from your point of view. I always liked the song. Now, I'll have to think a little more on a lot of things. I certainly didn't want to hurt your feelings by playing a song that depresses you. We do things unintentionally, and sometimes we don't think about the other person, or dog. I'll do better."

"OK," she said.

Chapter 9
Waking Up with Lucy

I had stiffened up so bad last night at bedtime my hips didn't want to work. It was strange that my knees felt ok. They're usually the problem. Lucy and I had walked over two miles a day for several days and I had forgotten to wear my knee braces each day, and still they didn't hurt. I told Lucy that we may have to skip tomorrow due to stiff hips. Her answer was to take a aspirin, which I did.

"Hey Mike," Lucy said sitting on my chest at 6:00 A.M. "How's the hips feeling this morning?"

"I just woke up," I said, "with a dog sitting on me. I don't know yet."

"Well, get up and check them out," she said.

"In a minute," I muttered.

"I'll lick your beard and face," she said.

"You better not," I said, as I started getting out of bed. "I don't like licking."

"I know you don't," she said with a little puppy grin. "That's why it's fun."

"If you ever want to go to the park again to walk, you won't," I said.

"Then get up and fix breakfast," she said. "I'm hungry, and so are Gertie and the cats. Plus, I need a bath."

"Leave me alone," I answered. "I don't want to get up."

Slurrrppp, went the big wet Dachshund kiss, right in the face, then she scampered down her bedside stairs.

"Lucy, you'll pay for that!" I shouted.

"SCORED!" she shouted back, heading for the living room.

Chapter 10
Lucy Wants to Bargain

At five o'clock Lucy the Dachshund brought me her harness. She tried to put it on herself. I gave it to the Wife and she struggled with Lucy. They both tried to get it on. I got my walking shoes, knee braces, and Lucy's pink leash. Now she went wild for sure. She wouldn't talk to me all the way to the park.

After a lap and a half, I shortened the leash to keep her right by my side. She was bad to pull, and today she was dragging me. She still wouldn't talk, but I knew she was listening. I kept telling her to 'walk with me, walk with me,' and about four times a lap I stopped, and told her to stop. I refused to move until she quit pulling and stood still. Then told her to 'GO.' We did that over and over. Lucy got better on each lap. We've done about three laps a day.

She kept looking up at me. "You're tired," I said. "Ain't you?"

"Nope," she said. "I was just checking on you, fat boy. I heard Grandma tell Caleb the last time he walked with us to watch you, and if you began to look peaked, to stop."

"Well, do I look peaked?" I asked.

"I don't know what it means," she said. "So I don't know."

"It means pale looking, heavy sweating, not being able to focus," I said. "Stuff like that."

"You're pumping water pretty good," she said. "But that's about it. Guess you're all right."

"I'll show you how all right, Miss Lucy," I said. "We're going another lap."

At the end of the fourth lap, I put her in the Excursion. "That was your best lap," I said. "People were noticing you."

"Who was the man and woman getting water at the cave? They said I was gorgeous," she said.

"I don't know them," I said. "But the woman with the baby was Marley, she works at City Hall."

"Was that her husband who sat on the track and played with me?" she asked.

"I'm not sure," I said. "It could have been."

"And the man who passed us said something," she said. "What did he say?"

"I don't know," I said. "It was in Spanish."

"I don't speak Spanish," she said, "just German, French, and English."

"I know," I said. "You've told me enough. Hey girl, we've walked five miles in three days. We're getting better."

"Then I get some bacon when we get home?" she asked.

"You heard what the vet said," I replied. "What about a carrot?"

"You eat a carrot," she said. "I want some bacon. We won't tell the vet."

"You think she won't know when she weighs you," I said.

"If I don't get some bacon," she said, "I'll give you a big slurp early in the morning."

"What about a piece of bell pepper?" I asked.

"Mike, your left arm is bleeding," she said. "What happened?"

"You've scratched me with your toenails," I said. "We're going tomorrow and get them cut."

"How many places are scratched and bleeding?" she asked.

"Three," I answered.

"Well, you're shooting for four," she said.

"I'll put you in a crate," I said.

"I'll howl till Grandma let's me out," she said. "Let's go to arbitration. Let Grandma decide."

"I might as well give you a piece."

Chapter 11

Lucy Runs Away

It was the weekend after Thanksgiving. I took Lucy and Gertie out in the yard to run and play for a little while. I'd left my phone in the house and stepped back inside to get it. Martha and I were sitting on the porch. I wasn't thinking about the dogs, when I heard a yip. Like one of them was hurt. I could see Gertie in the front yard. But Lucy wasn't around. I thought the yip had come from the side of the house. I told Martha to call Caleb from inside and help me find her because she wasn't coming when either Martha or I called her.

I thought something had gotten her. Caleb came out and he went around the house one way and I went the other. Both of us were calling as loud as we could. We didn't hear or see Lucy. She was only four months old and weighed about seven pounds. She'd make a good dinner for a lot of critters.

She finally came running from behind our neighbor's house, big smile on her face and jumped on me.

I just turned and went into the house.

A few days later Lucy climbs up on my chest before daylight.

"Hey Mike," she said. "You still mad at me?"

"Nah," I said. "But you need to be more careful about running away."

"I wasn't running away," she said. "I knew where home was."

"That's not the point," I said. "We're sitting on the porch, and hear you yip a few times. I thought you were still on the porch, but you were gone. There are huge timber rattlers in the woods around us. I killed a big one, and so did Caleb. Coyotes come down off the mountain at night, and I saw a big red fox walk across the back yard last week, and finally, there are huge hawks and owls. All would make an appetizer out of you."

"I was chasing a squirrel," she said. "I ain't scared of no coyote. I'll bite him."

"Sure you will." I said. "Didn't you hear us calling? Me, Martha, and Caleb were calling. You're supposed to come when called."

"Aww, Mike, that squirrel scent was too strong to stop," she said. "After he ran up a tree I came back."

"It's dangerous to run away," I said. "You could have run over a rattler, got lost, or have been stolen. You scared me."

"Well, you got even," she said. "You took me to the vet. They tied me up and amputated some more of my toes."

"Nobody tied you up," I said. "I was there, remember. They just clipped your nails. If you'd be still, they wouldn't even have to hold you. And you tried to bite Dr. "J". Next time they may put a strap on your nose."

"They better not." she said. "Did you see her push a pill down my throat with her finger? She might have had that finger in a cat's mouth."

"She told you she washed her hands," I said. "Most dogs eat those pills; they say they taste good. But not Miss Difficult."

"OK," she said. "Now, do I get a turkey leg for Thanksgiving?"

"No," I said. "Maybe you'll get a Milk Bone."

"Don't start trouble, Mike," she said. "I'll go sit in grandma's lap and look pitiful, she'll give me one. And you'll get slurrrped in the morning."

"I'm getting me another Dachshund," I said. "I want one that will mind."

"No you're not," she said. "I'll bite you on the toe. And I'll show it how to have fun. I'll teach it to jump on Gertie, run up and down grandma, and chase cats and squirrels."

Chapter 12
Christmas 2015

I had a booth at the "Small Town Christmas in the Country" event held each year on the first weekend of December in Cave Spring at Rolater Park. It's a huge event. There were somewhere around 140 vendors. During the first day my daughter and granddaughter brought Lucy by to see me. I could tell she was full of questions, and knew that later on that night she would unload. I was right.

"Hey Mike," said Lucy the Dachshund. "What was going on in the park? I never saw so many people."

For the next three nights I told her about Christmas. I read her the Christmas story from the book of Luke and from Matthew also. She asked a million questions. I found several Veggie Tales books that my grandchildren had at one time and gave her one. She could put the story together by just looking at the pictures, plus she was beginning to pick up a word now and then.

I read her most of the Bible stories that we teach small kids in Sunday school classes.

Lucy was sitting in front of the fireplace looking through her favorite book.

"You know my favorite Bible story, Mike," she said, putting the book down and climbing up into my lap.

"Don't have a clue," I said.

"The little shepherd boy knocking the big guy in the head with a rock," she said.

"David and Goliath," I said. "David used a slingshot to throw his rock."

"Will you teach me to use a slingshot?" she asked.

"Why?" I asked.

"You remember that Boxer Bulldog in the park that growled and scared me," she said.

"Yeah, I remember," I said. "Why?"

"Cause I'll have a surprise for him," she said.

"You sit in my lap and listen to me read the Bible to you every morning," I said. "Don't you remember it says to turn the other cheek?"

"Yeah, yeah, I remember," she said. "Then if he slaps you again, give him your cloak."

"Hey, that's good, Lucy," I said.

"Mike, what's a cloak?" she asked.

"It would be like one of your favorite dresses," I said.

"No, no, he ain't getting one of my dresses," she said. "Anyway, after that it didn't say anything else. That's when the rock flies. Then run up and bite him hard on the ear."

"You ain't listening," I said. "That big dog would bite you in half."

"Not if you're there," she said. "Mike, do dogs go to heaven?"

"I sure hope so, Lucy," I said. "I never thought about it before."

"I'll talk to you in the morning," she said, as she jumped down off my lap and headed for the bedroom.

Chapter 13
New Years 2016
Bones Are Good, but Not Good for You

"Lucy, where are you?" I called as I scanned the living room looking for her.

Lucy crawled slowly from behind the love seat next to the fireplace.

"I'm over here," she said.

"What are you doing?" I asked. "When I don't see or hear you, I get worried."

"You know what I'm doing," she said.

"No, I don't," I said. "Are you ok?"

"What was that you gave me to chew on?" she asked.

I had taken a left over grilled pork chop from the fridge. I cut the meat off the bone, and put it back to use in soup later this week. I separated the two sections of bone, and gave each Dachshund a section.

"It was a pork chop bone," I said. "Why?"

"Cause it's the best thing I've ever tasted in my whole life," she said, wagging her tail.

"Glad you liked it," I said.

"Why have you been holding out on me?" she asked.

"I'm not holding out," I said.

"Gertie said you were," answered Lucy. "She's been here a long time, and said you hardly ever give her a real bone. You give them to Sophie outside."

"Gertie's too fat," I said. "The vet says she's got to lose some weight, and even you are starting to get a belly."

"Mike, you eat bones and see how much you gain, ok," said Lucy. "You ain't exactly slim and trim yourself, big boy. Svelte, you ain't."

"I get your drift," I said. "But Sophie lives outside, and runs all the time. She can burn off leftovers."

"She's half Jack Russell and half Rat Terrier," said Lucy, raising her voice. "She's a bag of nerves."

"Ok, I'll tell you a secret," I said, "if you'll get over being mad."

"What is it?" she asked.

"When the weather gets warm, somebody is out by the pool grilling every weekend," I said.

"Them pork chop things?" she said.

"Yep, and ribs and other things too," I said. "But there's a problem, bones are not good for dogs. They can splinter and poke holes in your intestines causing a lot of pain, and maybe surgery. No vet recommends eating bones."

"When does that start?" she asked. "When does warm weather get here? I'll take my chances about getting holes in my gut. I'm not going to worry about it."

"Soon as the pool gets open," I said. "It will still be a few months. Can you swim?"

"Like a beaver," she said. "But I'll need a bathing suit."

"We'll get you one," I said. "I'll debone you some meat every now and then, but no more bones."

"Pink or light blue," she said. "You're doing better, Mike. Now, I want another bone."

"No," I said. "I shouldn't have given you the one I did."

Chapter 14
Lucy Will Do Anything for Toys

I had no intention of watching this game. But Lucy the Dachshund insisted. She's a big Alabama fan. But she wanted to see a Super Bowl. She'd heard about the half-time show, and all the commercials. I warned her about one of the commercials before it came on. I told her she wouldn't like it.

"Why do you think I won't like it?" she asked.

"Cause it's about Dachshunds," I said.

"Ok, there should be one about the best breed of dog," she said. "What's wrong with that?"

"It's what they have them do," I said. "They line up on one side of a field, a lot of them, and they run across the field to the waiting owners on the other side."

"What's wrong with that?" she asked.

"They have half a hot dog bun strapped to each side, and a wiener on top," I said. "Then when they get to their owners they jump up in their arms, with big smiles on their faces. The owners are dressed in mustard and cat-sup bottle costumes. It's a Heinz commercial."

"How embarrassing," she said. "I'd never dress like a hot dog."

"You wouldn't?" I asked.

"That's demeaning," she said. "Why do they do it?"

"I don't know," I said. "Maybe they get treats."

"Treats?" she asked. "What kind?"

"Probably all kinds," I said, "and toys too."

"With squeakers?" she asked.

"Is there any other kind?" I answered.

"On second thought, go sign us up," she said. "You can wear a catsup bottle."

"I don't think so," I said.

"Well, go get me some treats to eat while we watch the game," she said.

Chapter 15
Lucy Gets Surgery

Lucy had been mad at me and wouldn't speak for several days. I told her she needed to be getting over her mad spell. One day, she jumped up on the ottoman in front of me and unloaded.

"Mike, I'm minding my own business, you grab me up and away we go. I thought we were going to the park or maybe downtown to walk around and see folks. But, oh no, you take me to the place where they cut my toenails off, stick things in me, and poke pills down my throat."

"Those were shots," I said. "All puppies get a series of them so you can go to places like the park, or downtown, and not catch some disease."

"Well, they hurt," she says. "I don't want any more."

"You'd rather get sick?" I asked.

"No, I don't want to get sick," she said. "Let me finish."

"Go ahead," I said.

"When we get there," she said, "I think, *ok, I get stuck and nails cut, then we can go home.* But oh no, you give me to some guy and leave. He takes me and puts me in jail."

"It's not jail," I said. "It's a cage."

"And the difference is?" she wanted to know. "Anyway, I'm locked up for no reason, then after four or five hours they come and take me back to the room where you get stuck and they stab me again with one of your shots."

"That's just a needle," I said.

"Then I wake up back in my cell," she says, "with my belly cut open, two of my teeth were missing, and all my toenails cut off. And it hurts. Why did you have them do that to me?"

"Well, the two teeth were puppy teeth that hadn't come out," I said. "They would have become infected and you wouldn't have been able to eat treats. The belly cut was

34

to help you have a more fun-filled life. No puppies every year. You've seen the commercials on TV where dogs and cats are mistreated and have no owners. They're left in the pounds and sometime when they're not adopted they're destroyed. And after awhile the health of the mama dog can come into question. There are just too many dogs now. And Lucy, I just can't take care of more dogs, and I would worry about them. So now we can go places, and do things. Now you're a sport model."

"Sport model," she said. "This sport model wants a pretty collar, lots of trips downtown, some squeaky squirrels to play with and lots of treats."

"Sounds like a deal," I said. "Just get over being mad about it,"

"I will," she says. "You better tell me from now on what you're planning on doing to me...or I'll bite you."

Chapter 16
Lucy Goes Back to the Vet to Get Chipped

I called Lucy over and told her to jump up on the otto-man. She sat and looked at me for a long time. I had to break the sad news to her, and I sure did dread it.

"I don't like the way you're looking at me," she said. "I don't have to go back to the vet anytime soon, do I?"

"I'm afraid you do," I said.

"For what?" she asked.

"To get the sutures out, where they did your surgery," I answered.

"What's a suture?" she asked.

"Little strings tied together to get your stomach healed up," I said.

"Will it hurt?" she asked.

"Nah," I said, "just sting a little."

"And that's it," she said. "No shots or cutting my toe-nails off."

"Not sure about the nails," I said. "I did ask them to put a chip in you."

"WHAT is a chip?" she asked.

"It's like a name tag placed under the skin," I said. "So if you get lost some nice person can take you to any vet and they will know where to call me to come get you."

"Why don't you get one?" she asked.

"Wouldn't do any good," I said. "You don't have a phone to receive a call. All little boys and girls need to learn their address and phone number in case they get lost. Also their parents name. If you want to start talking to other people, then we can forget the chip."

"That's not going to happen," she said. "How do they put this chip under my fur?"

"With a needle," I said.

"I knew it," she said. "I'll bet it's a big one too."

"A little bigger than the one you get shots with," I said.

"The chip doesn't have 666 on it, does it?" she asked.

"No, it doesn't have 666," I said. "You're crazy!"

"Mike, you know all this is going to cost you," she said. "I want bacon and eggs, every morning for a week. You could have had the chip put in while I was asleep for my surgery. You forgot it, didn't you?"

"I know it's going to cost me," I said. "It already has, and yes I forgot it. I could just go to Collinsville and get me another Dachshund puppy that didn't talk."

"Don't threaten me buster," she said. "It's your fault, not mine."

On the way home from the vet she chastised me good.

"Mike, you said getting the stitches out wouldn't hurt."

"You didn't holler," I said, "but you sure did squirm."

"It was over before I could," Lucy said. "I got a question for you."

"What's that?" I asked.

"I came to live at your house the first of September," she said. "Right away you start dragging me to the vet who just loves to stick needles in me, and cutting my toenails off. I don't understand about her and my feet."

"You have to have your nails clipped," I said. "And you have to have your puppy shots. If you were a little girl person you would get just as many. Shots keep you from getting diseases and being sick."

"So many?" she asked. "It seems like we went every week."

"No," I told her. "We went three times till you finished your shots."

"Then you take me and they put me to sleep," she said. "They cut me open, cut off my toenails once again, and pull two of my teeth out. Today they take out stitches and stab me with a sixteen-gauge needle putting in a chip."

"You weren't stabbed," I said. "You never asked your question?"

"Are you through taking me to the vet?" she asked.

"For awhile," I said.

We were almost home before she said anything else.
"You better get me a treat when we get to the house!"
"Chicken jerky be ok?" I asked.
"That'll be fine."

Chapter 17
Lucy Wants her Ears Pierced

"Hey Mike," said Lucy the Dachshund. "Those little girls who rode to church with you this morning, then brought the cake to the house this afternoon, did you see their ears?"

"What about them?" I asked.

"They had shiny spots at the bottom of their ears."

"They were earrings, or rather posts." I said.

"Do they grow on their ears?" she asked.

"No, they attach with pins or small posts," I said. "Why do you ask?"

"Cause I want some in my ears," she said.

"You do," I said. "A Dachshund with her ears pierced. Ok, if that's what you want."

"What does pierced mean?" she asked.

"They poke holes in your ears," I said. "So the posts will go through."

"That's crazy," she said. "I've had enough holes poked in me."

"You can get one in your belly too," I said. "Or you can get one through your lip or nose. Let me get a needle and I'll fix you up right now."

"Hold up, Mike," she said. "I need to think about this. No more messing with my belly, or my lip and nose."

"You can also get a stud through your tongue," I said.

"Through the tongue!" she said. "How do you eat?"

"Got me," I said with a shrug. "Well, come on and we'll do the ears, and you can think about the other places."

"It's hard being a girl," she said, "isn't it?"

"I wouldn't know," I said. "Come on, let's get this over with. I've got a needle and some of Grandma's pearl posts."

"Mike, you touch me with a needle....I'll bite you!"

Chapter 18
Lucy's First Snow

I looked out the window and saw that it was snowing to beat the band. I always took the Dachshunds out for a pit stop when the mail ran.

"Come on, girls," I said. "It's mail call."

Both ran to the door. Lucy ran out on the porch and froze. Gertie did a U-turn and was back inside before the door closed. Sophie, the outside dog, was standing on the porch.

Walking down the steps, I turned and called to her.

"Come on, Lucy," I said. "Let's get the mail."

"Mike, what is that stuff?" she asked, standing on the top step.

"It's snow," I said. "Come on."

"What's snow?" she asked.

"It's just frozen rain," I said, walking down the drive way.

"Gertie ran back inside," she said.

"She's a big chicken," I said.

"I'm a chicken too," she said coming slowly down the steps.

"Mike, watch out!" she yelled. "That stuff is getting on you."

I looked back and saw Lucy running toward me as fast as her little legs would carry her. When she stopped she started biting at the flakes.

"What are you doing?" I asked.

"They're getting on me!" she yelled, "and they're cold."

"I told you it was frozen rain."

"C'mon Mike," she said looking up at me with fifty-cent sized flakes landing on her. "Let's get in the house."

When we got to the steps, she stood at the bottom till I was on the porch.

"That was close," she said as she shook the snow from

her back in front of the fireplace.

"I thought you were chicken," I said. "Were you coming to save me?"

"I sure was," she said. "I thought I could bite all those white things, but there were too many."

"That was nice, Lucy," I said. "Snow just makes you cold and wet, at least around here."

"I found that out," she said. "I won't rescue you no more when you go out in the snow."

"I bet you would," I said.

"Uh-huh," she said. "Sure I will. Rub a lamp, Deacon."

Chapter 19
Lucy Bites a Wasp

Goldie the Cat (my writing partner) batted a wasp down in the dining room. Lucy saw it and took off toward where it fell. I was yelling for her to leave it alone. She grabbed it up, I guess to deprive Goldie. She discovered that it doesn't take long for a Dachshund puppy to check out a wasp.

"Mike," she said. "You better stop laughing at me."

"I can't help it," I said. "You were jumping around like a bareback bronc in a rodeo. All stiff legged, back bowed, head down, you're funny."

"That thing bit me inside my mouth," she said. "You think it's funny."

"I told you to leave it alone," I said. "You didn't listen. Just like when you chased the squirrel."

"Hey, just cool it about the squirrel," she said. "That's old news. But me getting bit by a bug is not funny."

"Sure looked funny," I said. "You were hopping around like a rabbit all over the house."

"You'll think funny in the morning," she said. "I'm going to jump on you and give you some big wet Dachshund kisses before you wake up."

"You better not," I said. "I don't like being woke up with a dog licking my face. I'll ground you from the park, and from treats."

"Grandma will give me some," she said, "and make you take me to the park and downtown. Where did that yellow cat go? I'm going to chase her."

"You're fixing to get scratched," I said. "Goldie ain't scared of you."

"I ain't scared of her either," she said. "I don't like her anyway."

"Why?" I asked.

"Cause you let her go in the office when you're writing,"

she said, "and won't let me."

"My office is the only room on this floor with carpet," I said. "I'm afraid you'll have an accident. Plus, it's packed with all kinds of stuff. There's too much for you to leave alone."

"I promise," she said. "Let me in, and I'll be good."

"No," I said. "You got to get bigger, and older."

"That's it," she said jumping off the ottoman. "You're getting kisses at daylight, and a bit toe to boot."

"Go bite a wasp," I yelled as she headed for the kitchen.

Chapter 20
Easter 2016
Lucy Goes to the Church Easter Egg Hunt

"Hey Mike," said Lucy the Dachshund. "Can I have more ham?"

"You've had enough," I said, "and be quiet, somebody will tell the vet you got a piece of ham for Easter."

"It sure was good," she said. "Is that the ham you picked up downtown?"

"Yep," I said. "Activity committee was selling them for a fundraiser. I noticed it made you run in circles when I brought it home."

"It smelled so good," she said. "Mike, I had a good time hunting Easter eggs at the church today. But they weren't real eggs. I'll eat real ones."

"I know you will," I said, "but you're not supposed too. Not this time. You're supposed to see how many eggs you can find. If you eat some of them, you lose count."

"How many eggs did I find?" she asked.

"You found a bunch," I said. "It was nice of you to give them to the babies."

"Well, they couldn't hunt them too good," she said. "You can't eat them, and they didn't have squeakers."

"I know," I said. "I thought you looked real pretty today in your new Easter dress."

"Mike, it's church, you know," she said. "Don't you like to dress up every now and then when you go?"

"I think it's more important to just go," I said. "But yes, sometimes I do."

"Thanks, Mike," she said, "for telling me the Easter Story."

"You're welcome," I said. "I'm glad you liked it."

"Now how about a little more ham," she said.

Chapter 21
Lucy Wants to Go to the Ball Game

With the coming of April, it was time for baseball. I've been a season ticket holder for the Class 'A' Rome Braves since they came to town in 2003. I love to go.

On opening night as I returned home I knew Lucy would be mad. I knew she wanted to go, but dogs aren't allowed but one day a year. To make it worse, I was under doctor's orders to apply a cream to my old bald head twice a day for skin treatment, and it looked horrible. My hat wouldn't even cover where it ran down my face.

"Hey Mike," said Lucy the Dachshund. "Where ya been?"

"I told you I was going to the baseball game," I said.

"I wanted to go too," she said, "and you left me here. I was lonely."

"That's just separation anxiety," I said.

"What's that?" she asked.

"It's when your owner leaves you and you get all stressed out," I said. "Lots of dogs have it, especially Dachshunds."

"Well, I don't have any such thing," she said. "I just wanted to go. Will you take me next time?"

"I can't," I said. "Dogs aren't allowed.

"Ich mochte das ballspiel zu gehen," she said in German. *"Es ist nicht fair. Ich bin nicht irgenden hund."*

"Will you calm down," I said. "Quit speaking German. I can't understand a word."

After she calmed down a little, she looked up and said.

"Your head and face look awful."

"I know," I said. "I sit in the shade staying out of the sun until this medicine peels the bad places of my face and head."

"Sure looks bad now," she said. "You look like a freak of some kind. Have you ever thought of joining the circus?"

"Ha, ha," I said. "Ain't you the funny one?"

"I heard Caleb tell Grandma a dog threw out the first

pitch at Friday night's ball game," she said. "Is that true? You said dogs couldn't go."

"Well, sort of," I said.

"What do you mean, sort of?" she asked. "They either did or didn't."

"It was a person dressed up like a dog," I said.

"That's what I figured," she said. "Why do people dress up like dogs? That makes me mad. Dogs don't dress up like people. Remember the take a bite out of crime dog, trying to talk in a deep voice. How silly can you get?"

"That's McGruff," I said. "Kids love him, and he has a good message. I used to lead him around."

"Some people dress their dogs up like different historical or sports figures," I said. "Don't you remember the pictures I showed you on the internet?"

"I remember," she said. "I didn't think much of that either."

"I could dress you up like a person, or another dog breed," I told her.

"Don't even think about it," she said.

"A poodle," I said. "I could dress you like a poodle. We could glue a puffy ball on the end of your tail, and put cotton around your shoulders. You speak French, so it would be perfect."

"You want to get bit, don't ya," she said. "You can get bit quick trying to make me look like a poodle."

"I think poodles are cute," I said. "John Steinbeck, one of the greatest writers ever, had a poodle."

"Yeah, I know," she said. "His poodle was named Charlie, and he got to travel everywhere. I get to stay home, or go to the vet."

"You need to learn to behave," I said.

"I'm trying," she said. "Will you go by that lady's place where you got my Easter dress and get me some more cow tails and lamb's ears? They sure were good."

"Backyard Pet Boutique," I said. "Will you be good?"

"I won't bite you," she said. "But I still want to go places."

"Like where, besides the ball game?" I asked.

"Oh, I want to go to school with Caleb," she said, "and ghost hunting with Christy."

"All in good time," I said.

"Are you working on my book?" she asked.

"Sure am," I said. "Judith Johnson Frasure is going to do the illustrations."

"Whoa, Jack," she said. "I better get the right to pick the pictures and approve the illustrations."

"Well, of course, we wouldn't want it any other way," I said. "Judith is going to drop by the house when she gets a few done. Then you can see how good she is at art work."

"Sounds good," she said. "Let's have a treat toast to celebrate," she said.

"No," I said. "You're overweight. Doctor's orders."

"Grrrrrr, you'll be sorry!" she growled.

Chapter 22
Lucy Learns What Bees Can Do for People

"Hey Mike," said Lucy the Dachshund. "I thought we were going to the park and downtown for a good evening walk."

"There's a swarm of bees on a tree in front of the Old Church," I said.

"So," said Lucy. "They're just bugs. You scared of bugs, Mike?"

"I don't want to get stung," I said. "These bugs can hurt you, and I'm allergic to bee stings."

"What does stung feel like?" she asked.

"Like getting shots from the vet," I said.

"If a bug stings me," she said, "I'd bite him good."

"Lucy, there are thousands in a swarm," I said.

"Can't you kill them?" she asked.

"Sure you can," I said. "But we don't want to kill them. They pollinate our flowers and crops in the field so we can have good things to eat. A lot of bees are dying. We need all we can get."

"So we just leave them in the park," she said, "and forget walking."

"Oh no," I said. "A bee keeper will come and get them and put them in a hive."

"A what?" she asked.

"A hive is a house where bees can live," I said, "and make honey."

"Honey?" asked Lucy. "Bees make honey?"

"Yep," I said. "That's where it comes from."

"Why didn't you say that to start with," she said, "all that talking for nothing?"

"You keep sticking your nose in our rose bushes," I said, "you'll get to meet one up close and personal."

"I still ain't scared of no bee," said Lucy.

Chapter 23
Lucy Learns How Hateful Words Can Hurt

I woke up at six o'clock this morning with Lucy the Dachshund sitting on my chest.

"Hey, Mike," said Lucy the Dachshund. "You awake?"

"I am now," I replied.

"Good," she said. "I want to talk."

"Kind of figured," I said.

"Those kids in the park," she said, lying down on my chest. "They were mean. We were just walking by and they started pointing and laughing at me."

"I know," I said. "I heard them."

"We weren't bothering them or nothing," she said.

"I know," I said. "Sometimes people don't realize how hurtful they're being. Then other times they do it on purpose, to cause pain."

"I'm a Dachshund," she said, "not a sausage dog. I got long ears, short legs, and a pretty good sniffer."

"I understand," I said.

"So what's funny about that?" she asked.

"Nothing to me," I said. "I like you just like you are."

"I wanted to bite one little boy," she said. "You should have turned me loose and I would have. It hurt my feelings so bad."

"Mike, I've always been proud I was a Dachshund. While they were laughing at the 'weenie dog', I was wishing I was a poodle or cocker spaniel."

"You just need to ignore them," I said. "If you bite somebody, they'll call the dog catcher to come get you."

"I'll bite him too," she said.

"Then he'd put a noose around your neck and take you to doggie jail."

"Wouldn't you come and get me?" she asked.

"I'd try," I said, "if they'd let me."

"I got to think about this some more," she said as she

climbed down her steps.

"You can't bite everybody," I yelled after her.

"No, but I can bite you," she said. "How about getting up and fixing breakfast. I want chopped chicken from a can this morning. Not the dry stuff in the vet's specimen cup."

I could hear her in the kitchen singing. 'She's in the jailhouse now. She's in the jailhouse now. I told her once or twice. Quit biting people, and try to be nice.'

Chapter 24
Lucy Finds Out Gertie and Sophie Go to the Vet Also

"Hey Mike," said Lucy the Dachshund. "You took Gertie and Sophie to the park yesterday and left me here. Why would you do such a thing? It hurt my feelings."

"To the park," I said. "We didn't go to the park. We went to the vet."

"To the vet," she said. "Gertie told me...oh I get it, she fooled me."

"She must have," I said, "cause we didn't go to the park."

"Why did they go to the vet?" she asked. "They're not sick."

"Gertie was due for a check-up," I said. "We got her a three-month flea pill, and a mani pedi. She was so good."

"Yeah, yeah, she's old and fat," said Lucy. "I ain't that easy."

"She had lost a pound," I said. "To her a pound is a lot."

"She's still fat," Lucy said. "What did they do to white dog?"

"She got a haircut and a bath," I said. "Plus she got two shots and a flea pill."

"Shots," she said. "Glad you left me here. I am not getting any more shots. In fact, I will not go to the vet anymore."

"You're going next week," I said, "to get you a mani pedi and get weighed. You're beginning to look a little pudgy yourself. Plus, you get a flea pill too."

"Impossible," she said. "You share your dinner with big ole Gertie, when all I get is a thimble full in a specimen cup. There's no way to get fat. I ain't going, and I don't want her running her finger down my throat pushing a pill."

"Yes, you are," I said. "Dr. Johnson has already been through that part about fingers in your throat. You need the pill, and you're going to get it."

"Oh, it's biting time again," she started singing as she headed for the kitchen. "It won't be long before its biting time."

"You're still going!" I yelled after her.

Chapter 25
Lucy Has Big Dreams

"Hey Mike," said Lucy the Dachshund. "Did you see the audience I drew yesterday when we were downtown?"

"How could I help," I said, "with you showing off every where we walked. Don't let it go to your head."

"I was thinking," she said. "After my book is a big seller, maybe we should make a TV cartoon movie. I'd be the star."

"Big seller, huh," I said. "You think it'll be a big seller. Aren't you putting the cart before the horse?"

"Yep," she said. "I know I'm better looking than fat old Garfield the Cat, and Snoopy too."

"You eat like Garfield," I said, "and have an imagination like Snoopy."

"So, you'll do it," she said.

"What if the movie people don't see your true potential?"

"You planning on getting blind ones, Mike," she said. "Then they can feel the potential on their ankles."

"Good grief," I said.

"Hey Gertie," she yelled heading to the bedroom. "I'm going to make a movie. You want to be in it?"

Chapter 26
Memorial Day

"Hey Mike," said Lucy the Dachshund. "Can we have Memorial Day every weekend?"

"Sorry," I said. "It doesn't work that way. It's only celebrated on the last Monday in May. Why do you want to do have it every weekend?"

"I like the menu," she said. "The can of chopped chicken was good. The Boston Butt was out of this world, the watermelon was cold and sweet, and Gertie and I love getting a piece of bacon each morning. This was a great weekend."

"Shhhh," I said. "Grandma doesn't know I gave you those things. Plus, Mary at the vet's office will be telling the vet on us. You need to learn to keep your big mouth shut. You can have watermelon anytime. And you only had a small piece of Boston Butt, and I shouldn't give you bacon."

"Any of the Boston Butt seems like a lot," she said. "If all you had was dry dog food day after day, you'd want more Memorial Days too."

"Memorial Day is not about Bar BQ and eating," I said. "It's a national holiday to remember the brave men and women who gave up their lives so we could be free, and have holidays."

"Did some brave dogs give up their lives too?" she asked.

"They sure did," I answered. "A lot of brave dogs died in battle."

"Wow," she said. "That's worth celebrating, how about another piece of bacon?"

"In a little over a month we'll have another holiday," I said. "The 4th of July."

"What's that?" she asked.

"It's when we celebrate the birth of our nation," I said, "when a group of colonies declared their independence from Great Britain, and became the United States."

"Do me and Gertie get bacon?" she asked. "We always celebrate better with bacon."

"We'll see," I said. "It would be nice if you'd behave a little better."

"Bacon every morning," she said, "and you got a deal."

"Not going to happen," I said. "You'd gained another half pound on our last visit to the vet."

"Dang, another month of dog food pellets from a specimen cup," she said. "I may give you my declaration of no more dry stuff without bacon."

Chapter 27
Lucy Steals a Sausage Ball

"Hey Mike," said Lucy the Dachshund. "Why are you up so early this morning?"

"It's my Sunday to fix breakfast for the Sunday school class," I said. "We rotate every week, and it's my week."

"What are you fixing?" she asked. "It sure does smell good."

"We started off with just donuts and coffee," I said. "Now we've added a little more. Each person has their own specialty."

"Why did you keep adding?" she asked.

"When it was just the senior class, it didn't matter so much," I said. "Then the vans started bringing in little kids for church. We were worried they may not have eaten breakfast. So, we feed them too."

"Mike, that's awful nice," she said.

"It's not a big church congregation," I said. "Sometimes there are a couple of van loads of kids, plus the youth. We just feed whoever shows up."

"What smells so good?" she asked again.

"Sausage balls," I said. "I usually do a lot of them, and chicken nuggets too."

"Can I have some?" she asked.

"No," I said. "They're for the kids at the church."

"Can I have just one?" she pleaded.

"No, I told you who they were for," I said. "I'll give you a piece of cantaloupe from the fruit bowl. You don't need the sausage ball. It has cheese in it, and is breaded with flour."

"What about a chicken nugget?" she asked.

"No," I said. "They're breaded too."

"You're starving me to death," she said. "Why do they smell so good?"

"When I take the sausage balls from the oven, I put the

nuggets in the grease," I said. "It gives them flavor."

As I was scooping up the nuggets and sausage balls, I dropped one on the floor. Lucy grabbed it and headed for parts unknown. I followed her into the bedroom, where she had run under the bed.

"Lucy," I said, "it's not good for you. Give it back and I'll give you a piece of jerky, or a cow's tail."

"Rub a lamp, Deacon," she said. "I'm keeping this. It's a little hot now, but will cool off in a minute. Then it's down the hatch."

"You'll be sorry," I said.

"No I won't," she said. "You were being selfish. You knew it made me hungry, and could have offered me a cow tail before you dropped the sausage ball."

I went back to the kitchen and finished packing my breakfast. She was right. I could have given her something that wouldn't be bad for her, but didn't. I can't stay mad at her.

Chapter 28
Baby Announcement

"Lucy, we need to talk." I said.

"Can it wait?" she said. "I'm busy."

"You're not busy," I said. "You're sleeping."

"That's busy, Mike," she said. "Don't you know how important sleep is to puppies?"

"Yes I do," I said, "and that's what I want to talk to you about."

"What?" she said. "You want to talk about sleep. Just be quiet and I'll show you how it's done."

"No, I want to talk about puppies," I said.

Lucy sat up and looked into my eyes for a long time.

"Ok, big boy," she said. "You got my attention. What's up?"

"We're getting another Dachshund puppy," I said. "I will pick her up this coming Friday."

"You're kidding, aren't you," she said, "and it's not funny."

"Not kidding at all," I said. "She's a little eight-week old blond Dachshund."

"So, where do I go," she asked, "to another home or to the pound for adoption?"

"What?" I asked. "You don't go anywhere buster, you stay right here with me."

"You'll love the new puppy more than me," she said. "I'll be second Dachshund."

"Wrong again," I said. "Lucy, Grandma and I are dog and cat lovers. We've had all kinds of dogs and cats our entire lives. Gertie is getting old. I hope she's with us for many years, but she doesn't get around too good. I got you for Grandma, so if anything did happen to Gertie, she would have another Dachshund to love. I didn't know you were going to be so doggone unique. Now, I can't stand the idea of you growing up without another Dachshund to share your experiences, to have someone to play with, to wrestle, and to chase.

Gertie isn't able to do those things. I think you will enjoy having a baby sister to play with."

"Well, Mike," she said. "You make it sound interesting. I'll have to think about it. But I'm willing to give it a try."

"That's my girl," I said. "Just for the record, you're not allowed to teach her bad things."

"Mike, I'm crushed," she said. "I would never think of teaching a puppy to misbehave. You've hurt my feelings."

"Uh-huh," I said. "I'm warning you. I'll be watching."

Chapter 29
Ginger Is Her Name

"Hey Mike," said Lucy the Dachshund. "What did you name the blond?"

"Ginger," I said. "My daughter is calling her Gigi."

"Gigi," said Lucy, "that's not bad. In the movie I think Leslie Caron played Gigi, and did a great job. She was into everything."

"I remember Maurice Chevalier," I said. "But how did you know? Did you see the movie?"

"I don't know," she said. "I don't remember seeing it, but I know all about it."

"How do you know about it?" I asked.

"I told you I don't know," she said. "Same way I can speak out loud. Don't have to think my thoughts like Snoopy or Garfield."

"Think your thoughts?" I asked.

"You know, in their comic strips, their thoughts appear above their heads," she said.

"Ok, now I get it." I said. "Do you like the blond girl?"

"I think she's fine," she said. "I do like Ginger better. You know she's gorgeous, don't you, almost as much as I am."

"Yes, I know she's gorgeous," I said, "and Ginger is her name."

"I think we'll make a fine pair," she said, "just as soon as I get her trained."

"Yeah, you better be careful about training her," I said.

"Oh Mike, have some faith," she said. "I've got that danged movie stuck in my head. See what you done."

"What movie?" I asked.

"Gigi," she said. "*Le Crime D'Amour oublie.*"

"What does that say?" I asked. "I don't speak French."

"Ask Chevalier," she said. "It's one of his quotes. It's hard to believe an old man is not as smart as his dog."

"That's all the bacon you get, smarty pants," I said. "And Maurice is dead."

Chapter 30
Lucy Wants a Reward

"Hey Mike," said Lucy the Dachshund. "Are you going to Rome again today?"

"Yep," I said. "I got to go by the grocery and pick up a few things."

"You know I've spent a week training your blond girl," she said.

"You mean Ginger?" I asked.

"Yep," she said. "The one and only, and she learns fast."

"I think so," I said. "She's growing too. Why are you telling me all this?"

"Cause I think I need a little reward for working so hard with her."

"Oh, you do," I said. "I asked you to find out if she likes it here. Did you?"

"Her English is pretty rough," said Lucy. "She's fluent in French, and I'm rusty. There's nobody to practice with. Gertie only speaks German. But I'm trying. How about give a girl a break?"

"What kind of reward?" I asked.

"I been dreaming about some cow tails and lamb ears," she said. "Would you pick me up some while you're in Rome?"

"I'll think about it," I said. "I will if I have time."

"Listen Mike," she said. "I can tell Frenchie you'll take her to the vet and get her shot, chipped, and they'll cut her toes off."

"She's already had her first shots," I said, "and her nails clipped."

"Please, Mike," Lucy whimpered. "It's been a long time, and I'll be extra good. No squirrel chasing, no following Sophie down the hill."

"No biting?" I asked.

"Ok," she said, hanging her head. "No biting."

"You have to share with Gertie and Ginger," I said. "Is

that understood?"

"Deal," she said.

Three hours later after stopping at the Backyard Boutique and getting cow tails, lamb ears, and some bully
sticks I came in the house, and here Lucy came.

"Did you get them, Mike?" she asked.

"Yep, sure did," I said. "Remember you said you'd share."

"Right," she said, grabbing two cow tails and heading
for the bedroom. "Rub a lamp, Fat Boy, hide and watch."

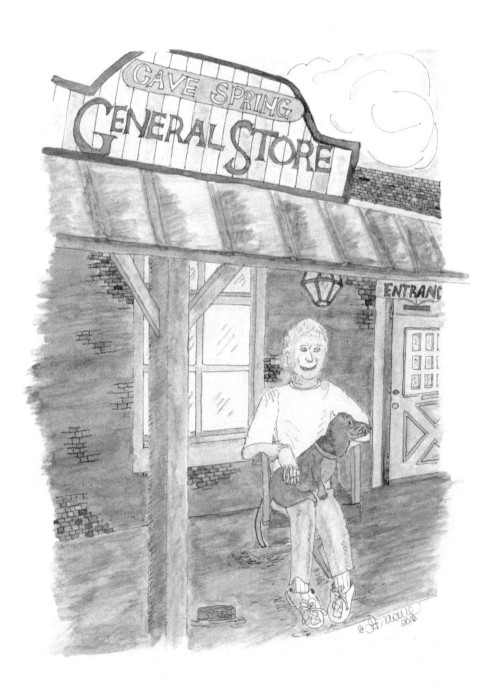

Chapter 31
4th of July Celebration
Lucy Meets Mr. Charles at the General Store

"Hey Mike," said Lucy the Dachshund. "I've never seen this many people in one place. What are they doing?"

"It's July 2nd," I said. "It's Saturday, Cave Spring will shoot their fireworks tonight. We usually do it on the 3rd because Rome does theirs on the 4th. We'll have over ten thousand people in town by dark."

"Looks like there's ten thousand here now," she said.

"A lot of folks come early to let the kids wade in the creek," I said. "Plus, all the pavilions and picnic tables in the park are full. The cave and pool are open, and there is a big car show in front of City Hall."

"I think a lot of folks are just walking around like we are," she said, "just looking."

"Yes," I said. "It's hot. Let's try and find some shade."

We looked at all the cars in the car show. I picked Lucy up so she could see inside. She picked out a red Mustang as her favorite. I liked a 1951 Mercury. After we finished with the show, we headed downtown. When we got to the General Store, I found a seat under the porch in the shade with the owner, Charles Ledbetter.

"Mike, does your little dog want some water?" Charles asked.

"I wouldn't think so, Charles," I said. "We've only been downtown for an hour or so."

Charles went into the store and brought a bowl of water for Lucy. She jumped right on it. Then he picked her up and held her in his lap.

"Mike, I think the asphalt is burning her feet," he said.

We stayed at the General Store for about thirty minutes before heading back to the Excursion. Lucy went to the door of the wrong car a couple of times. I had kept her in the grass as much as possible, but could tell she was glad to get to the car. That night we watched the fireworks from the front porch. Lucy had told Gertie and Ginger what the fireworks was all about. She explained Independence Day to them and the cats. I just don't know what she told them.

"Hey Mike," she said the next day. "Mr. Charles was nice to me. My feet were hot, and I was thirsty."

"How did you like all the celebrating?" I asked.

"I loved it," she said, "all but one thing."

"Everybody in the park was grilling," she said, "and I didn't get any."

"You're in luck," I said. "We'll be firing up the grill today and tomorrow."

"Chicken?" she said, with a big grin on her face.

"Yep, we'll be cooking chicken," I said, "among other things."

"My favorite," she said. "Boy, Frenchie is going to love this day."

Chapter 32
Lucy Goes to the Dentist

"Hey, Mike," said Lucy the Dachshund. "Thanks for the piece of bacon his morning, it sure was good."

"Glad you liked it," I said. "I think that was Ginger's first time to have bacon. Just remember, don't advertise, your vet reads my page. As does Grandma, and hundreds of other Dachshund lovers. They will all jump on me if they think you're getting to much bacon."

"I don't care who sees my comments," Lucy said. "You said I was finished going to the vet for awhile."

"No," I said. "I told you that you didn't have to go as much. Ginger goes for final puppy shots next week and you're going to get your nails trimmed."

"I don't want to," she said. "It hurts."

"You seem to have trouble chewing too," I said. "She needs to check your teeth and gums, and getting a mani pedi don't hurt."

"I don't have a problem chewing," she said. "She'll stick her fingers in my mouth."

"She has already told you she washes them a lot," I said. "Vets have lots of roles. In this case, she's a dentist. Taking care of your teeth is important, especially as much as you like to eat."

"I ain't going," she said.

"Yes, you are," I said, "enough of that nonsense. How are you and Ginger getting along? Y'all run and play all day."

"Oh yeah," she said. "Frenchie is a blast. I'm glad she came to live with us. When are you going to take us to the park? She's never been."

"I've been thinking about it," I said. "I wish you'd quit calling her Frenchie."

"Her accent is getting better," said Lucy. "It's still distinctive though. You know, Mike, if Frenchie and I were people, like some of the ladies you read to me about on your Facebook page, we would ROCK downtown Rome. I don't know if we would be downtown chicks, or uptown girls. But we'd be hard to keep up with."

"I have no doubt about it," I said. "You know what? Uptown girls go to the dentist and keep their teeth looking nice."

"Don't try to trick me, Mike," Lucy said.

"What did you think of Judith?" I asked.

"Wow, those sketches look just like me," she said. "The one already colored was great, didn't you think so?"

"I did," I said. "I almost forgot. Caleb wants you to go hunt Pokemons with him."

"Oh yeah," she said. "I'd love to go. I'll bite them Pokey things."

"Pokemons."

"Whatever," she said. "They're bit."

Chapter 33
Lucy and the Gander

"Hey Mike," said Lucy the Dachshund. "How you feeling after our evening walk yesterday?"

"I'm fine," I said. "How are you? You were panting on that last lap, and for thirty minutes after we got home."

"It was hot out there," she said. "I wasn't by myself, though. You were sweating like a mill hand."

"How do you know how a mill hand sweats?" I asked.

"From the book you're writing about working in the mill," she said. "You read out loud when you're re-writing."

"It's a habit," I said. "I want to hear how it sounds. I can tell if it flows like I want it to."

"Did you read my book out loud?" she asked.

"Several times," I said, "and I was sweating like a mill worker yesterday. It was 95 degrees when we came by the bank."

"Mike, what was wrong with that goose that tried to bite me?" she asked.

"That was a big old gander," I said. "You ran at him, and he ran back at you. He ain't scared of you, but you sure looked like you were scared by the way you ran."

"Well, would you want to get bit by a duck?" she asked.

"Goose," I said, "the other one that got after you was a mama duck. Didn't you see her babies?"

"Thought you said it was a gander," Lucy said.

"I did," I said. "A gander is a daddy goose."

"I saw the baby ducks," Lucy said. "I just wanted to play with them."

"There were baby geese at the lake also," I said. "Mama and Papa don't want dogs around."

"I don't know why," she said. "I just wanted to play a little."

"They didn't know what you wanted," I said. "I'm sure

they thought you might hurt them. Then they'd hurt you. All mamas take care of their babies, and they will bite you if you get too close."

"The cave water felt good after a mile," she said. "I love standing in an inch or two. Sure makes sore feet feel good."

"I could hear your nails clicking on the cement," I said. "You know what that means."

"Negative," she said. "You can take Frenchie, I'll stay with Grandma."

"They'll have to be cut," I said. "Your feet could get infected if they keep turning under, especially the dew claws."

"I'm not going," she said.

"No more going to the park," I said. "No more baby ducks and geese, robins and squirrels. No more cave water and getting to stand in it. No more of people telling you how gorgeous you are, and petting you. No more little kids making over you, or watching the trout feed in the Cave Lake. Boy, Ginger is going to love coming to the park with me."

"Mike, don't try to pull that stuff on me," she said. "I'll give you a big Dachshund kiss when you ain't looking."

Chapter 34
Lucy Scares Ginger

"Hey Mike," said Lucy the Dachshund. "Make that woman turn off the vacuum thing."

"You mean the housekeeper?" I asked. "I don't think so."

"We're afraid it'll suck us up inside," she said, "and we couldn't get out."

"It's not going to suck you up inside," I said.

"How do you know?" she asked.

"Cause you're too big," I said.

"Even if I am too big," she said, "it would hurt pulling on my skin trying to get me inside."

"No, it won't," I said, reaching for Lucy. "Here, I'll hold you and we'll put the vacuum hose up against you, and you can see for yourself."

"No, you won't," she said running for the front bedroom. "You grab me and I'll bite you good."

"Where's Ginger?" I asked.

"Under the bed hiding with me and the cats," she said.

"How cozy," I said. "See, y'all can get along when you want too."

"They're at one end of the bed, and we're at the other," she said, "everybody's scared."

"I don't know why," I said. "You're all too fat to go up a vacuum hose."

"Are you sure?" she asked.

"Yep, I'm sure," I said.

"Well, Frenchie is scared to death," she said. "I better stay here with her."

"I think you told Ginger all that to scare her," I remarked.

"Mike, I wouldn't do that to Frenchie," she said.

"Yes, you would," I said, "and it isn't nice to scare your little sister. I'm going to tell them to mop good under the bed."

"Mike, you need a good biting," she said. "Frenchie and I are going to nail you good."

"Ginger," I said, "not Frenchie. Come on and bite me now."

"We will later," she said.

"Are you chicken, Lucy?" I asked.

"Frenchie," said Lucy, "Mike said we were too big to go up the vacuum hose, but it could pull all our fur off, so stay hid."

"I did not say that," I said, "you quit scaring your sister."

Chapter 35
Lucy Turns One Year Old

"Hey Mike," said Lucy the Dachshund. "What are you up to this morning?"

"You mean after you woke me up at daylight," I said. "Nothing. I was sleeping."

"You been pretty busy, huh," she said.

"When I get up I have my morning chores," I said. "I have to do laundry, feed animals, take out garbage, grab the newspaper from the box, just the same stuff I do every day. Why are you being so nice? You don't care what I do every morning, as long as you get fed."

"Yes I do," she said. "You take good care of us."

"Uh-huh," I said. "Let's hear it."

"Do you know what today is?" she said.

"Sure," I said. "It's Wednesday."

"No, the date," she said.

"Yep, it's the 20th of July," I said. "What does that mean?"

"It means tomorrow is the 21st," she said.

"Ok, you can count," I said. "Most dogs can't."

"Tomorrow is my birthday," she said. "I'll be ONE year old. We've had a good year, haven't we Mike?"

"Yes, we have," I said. "Why tell me today?"

"Cause you got things to do today," she said.

"What?" I asked.

"Do you need your note pad?" Lucy asked, jumping all around and running in circles.

"I'm good," I said.

"To start with," she said, "I want bacon in the morning for breakfast, and more than one slice. Cook some for old Gertie and Frenchie too. Then, we want that soft food in a pouch, no dry stuff tomorrow. We took a vote. At lunch, we decided that we wanted at least two cans of chopped chicken, not sliced or chunked. You understand!"

"Yep," I said. "You want it stirred, not shaken. I've heard that before."

"You're crazy," she said. "Then, go by Backyard Boutique and get lots of treats. Cow tails, lamb ears, pig snouts and any other treats you see that we may like. Get lots of toys with squeakers for me and Frenchie. Plus, I want a new outfit."

"Is that all?" I asked.

"Yep," she said. "We're gonna Par-ty."

"We have to get Ginger her final shots," I said. "You both get a mani-pedi for your birthday. Then I have a council meeting at 6:00 p.m."

"You're not going to celebrate my first birthday?" she asked with her face drooping. "That's mean."

"We're going to celebrate like a rock star," I said. "You're not going to just gorge all day. I was thinking about a walk in the park in the morning, and then walking around downtown."

"After bacon?" she asked. "And will you tell me happy birthday a lot."

"I will, just as soon as you wake me in the morning."

"Lucy girl, you've come a long way this first year," I said. "Do you have any plans for year two?"

"Mike, I still have a lot to learn," she said. "Even the things I know, I need to increase my knowledge about."

"We're always learning," I said. "Are you saying you intend to continue your schooling?"

"I am," she said, "if you'll continue to teach me. I can't just register for classes or go to school. No one believes I can talk, and if I did talk in front of someone, I'd be in a lab somewhere, living in a crate before you could say Jack Robinson.

Then Dr. 'Better Than You' would start poking me with all kind of things, and eventually come up with the idea to cut my neck open and look at my vocal cords.

So Mike, I'm just your little Chocolate Dachshund, who will talk to no one but you. I hope that's all right."

"It's fine," I said. "Most folks think I'm nuts when I tell them you can talk, but they like your stories and antics."

"Well, Mike," she said, "I sometimes think you're a couple fries short of a happy meal. But that just helps me. As long as folks think you're making this up cause you're a writer, it's fine with me."

"I understand," I said. "Let them wonder. Those that believe in Santa know you can talk. The others have gotten too old."

"Mike, do you remember the bone I dug up in the park?" she asked. "The one you said looked like a finger bone."

"Sure do," I said. "I gave it to the police department and they sent it to the Crime Lab to find out if it was human or not. If it is human, it's awful old."

"Well I been thinking about that," Lucy said. "You know Pookie, the ghost Cat, has been following us around a lot in the park. She has also come here to the house on several occasions. I was thinking that she and Abigail might be able to shed a little light on the finger."

"You may be right," I said. "Your theory is they may have been in the park and saw what happened."

"And if they didn't," Lucy said, "some of the other permanent residents of downtown Cave Spring could be witnesses or have information."

"Brilliant deduction Dr. Holmes," I said.

"Thank you, Watson," she said. "So Mike, can we work on the case. I think it would be fun."

"Lucy," I said, "when you start investigations, all kinds of unexpected things pop up, even without getting ghosts to help. Are you sure?"

"I'm sure," she said.

"Ok," I said, "deal me in."

"I love you, Mike," said Lucy the Dachshund.

"I love you too, Lucy," I said rubbing her head and scratching hound dog ears.

About the Author

Mike Ragland was born and raised in Lindale, GA where he attended and graduated from Pepperell Schools.

After graduating from Pepperell High in 1963, he joined the Navy and was assigned to the submarine *The USS Chopper* (SS-342) and served from '63 to '67. During that time he served in the north Atlantic, Mediterranean, South America and throughout the east coast and Gulf of Mexico.

When Mike rejoined civilian life, he worked briefly laying carpet and was fired the day he planned to resign to join the Rome Police Department, where he served 40 years and retired as a Major. As a member of the force, he served as a motorcycle officer, patrol Sergeant, Shift Commander, and Captain in Charge of Detective Bureau. He also served as Juvenile Officer, as a liaison officer to Juvenile Court and Training Officer until 1999 when he was promoted to Major. As Major, he rotated serving the three major bureaus of the Police Department: Operations, Administration and Support Services. During that time he was also the principal grant writer for the Police Department, bringing in many Federal and State grants to secure police officer jobs, positions, and equipment, including the *"Call to Duty Monument"* that stands in front of the Rome Police Department today. He now serves as Councilman for the City of Cave Spring.

Mike was married to Martha Highfield on August 23, 1968, and they have one daughter, Bekki Ragland Fox, and two grandchildren, Caleb and Mattie Parris. He is an avid Crimson Tide and NASCAR fan. A much loved speaker and writer in Northwest Georgia. Mike is devoted to writing full times since his retirement from the Police Department in April of 2007. He and his wife currently live in Cave Spring, GA along with three aggravating cats and three dachshunds.

His previous books are: *Bertha, Legend of the Courage Wolf,* and *A Time to Gather Stones.*

Mike can be reached at mikeragland6@gmail.com.

an old man and his dog . . .
someone to talk to . . .

CPSIA information can be obtained
at www.ICGtesting.com
Printed in the USA
LVOW06s0839131116
512663LV00005B/5/P